THE BLIND MEN AND THE ELEPHANT

To Caroline

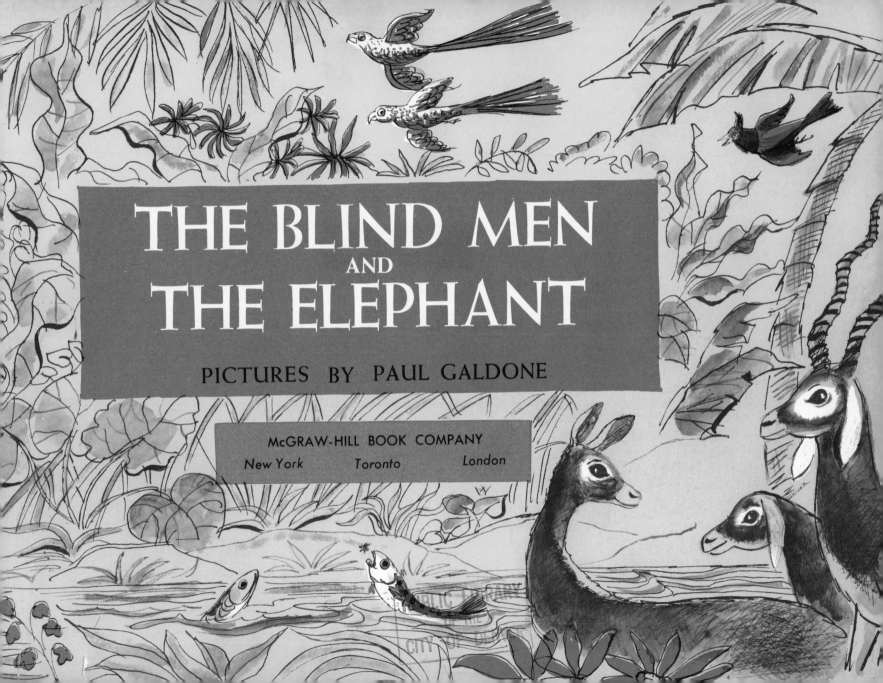

THE BLIND MEN
AND
THE ELEPHANT

PICTURES BY PAUL GALDONE

McGRAW-HILL BOOK COMPANY

New York   Toronto   London

Copyright © 1963 by Paul Galdone

Library of Congress Catalog Card Number: 62-20729
Book designed by Paul Galdone
Printed in the United States of America

THIRD PRINTING

It was six men of Indostan
     To learning much inclined,
Who went to see the Elephant
     (Though all of them were blind),

That each by observation
Might satisfy his mind.

The First approached the Elephant,
  And happening to fall
Against his broad and sturdy side,
  At once began to bawl:
"Bless me! but the Elephant
  Is very like a wall!"

The Second, feeling of the tusk,
    Cried, "Ho! what have we here,
So very round and smooth and sharp?

"To me 'tis mighty clear
This wonder of an Elephant
Is very like a spear!"

The Third approached the animal,
  And happening to take
The squirming trunk within his hands,
  Thus boldly up and spake:

"I see," quoth he, "the Elephant
Is very like a snake!"

The Fourth reached out his eager hand,
And felt about the knee.
"What most this wondrous beast is like
Is mighty plain," quoth he;

" 'Tis clear enough the Elephant
Is very like a tree!"

The Fifth, who chanced to touch the ear,
Said, "E'en the blindest man
Can tell what this resembles most;
Deny the fact who can,

"This marvel of an Elephant
Is very like a fan!"

The Sixth no sooner had begun
About the beast to grope,
Than, seizing on the swinging tail
That fell within his scope,

"I see," quoth he, "the Elephant
    Is very like a rope!"

And so these men of Indostan
Disputed loud and long,
Each in his own opinion
Exceeding stiff and strong,
Though each was partly in the right,
And all were in the wrong!